DIRT BIKE AT

WRITTEN BY L.A. Fielding

ILLUSTRATED BY Victor Guiza

Library and Archives Canada Cataloguing in Publication

Fielding, L. A. (Lawrence Anthony), 1977-, author
Dirt Bike at Badlands / written by L.A. Fielding ; illustrated by Victor Guiza.

(The X-tails)
Issued in print and electronic formats.
ISBN 978-1-928199-10-6 (paperback).

I. Guiza, Victor, illustrator II. Title. III. Series: Fielding, L.A. (Lawrence Anthony), 1977- . X-tails.
PS8611.I362D57 2016 jC813'.6 C2016-903594-8 C2016-903595-6

The X-tails Enterprises
Prince George, BC Canada

Printed in Canada

Design and text layout by Margaret Cogswell
www.spiderbuddydesigns.com

To Sean Edzerza. Thanks for inspiring me with your dirt biking adventures at Badlands!

MEET THE X-TAILS!

The smart and responsible lion who is the natural leader of the X-tails. He is a master at solving problems and can fix almost anything. Wisdom loves to "ROOaaaRRRR!" when he is having fun.

CHARM

The cute and bubbly kangaroo. She loves the spotlight and performing at contests in front of big crowds. Her kangaroo legs are perfect for jumping high and pedaling fast. When Charm is really happy, you will see her **HOP** around or **THUMP** her foot with a big smile.

CRASH

The clumsy, messy, and very goofy hippo. Crash usually finds himself in all sorts of trouble and is thankful that his X-tail friends are always there when he needs them. You can't help but laugh with Crash at the many silly things he does, especially when he bellows

"GAAAWHOOOOOMPHAAAAA!"

FLIGHT

The strong and fearless rocker gorilla. Flight not only plays the air guitar but also loves to play on any jump he can find. Although he is really big and hairy, this gorilla is a gentle giant. You know Flight is ready for air time when you hear him grunt

**"OOOHHHH,
OOOHHHH,
OOOHHHH!"**

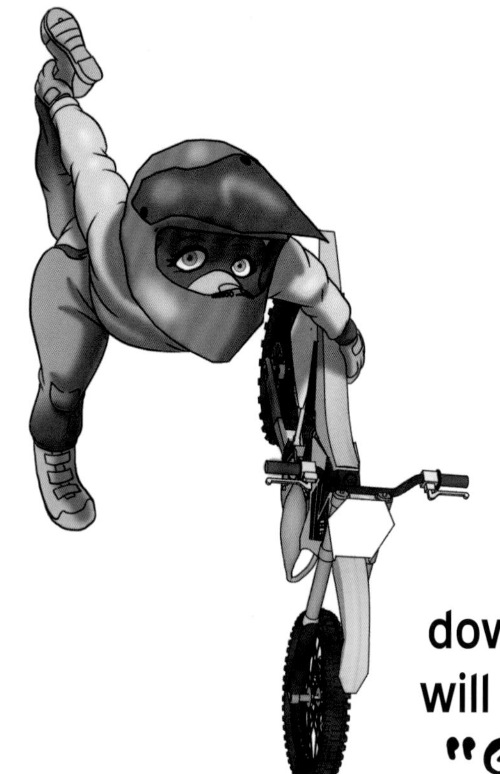

Dazzle

The tough and brave bear who is a tomboy at heart. The boys have difficulty keeping up with Dazzle. And good luck trying to slow her down! She has a big grin, and you will often hear her friendly growl, "GRRRRR!"

Mischief

The practical joker of the bunch. You know Mischief is up to something sneaky when you see his mischievous grin. He is a little short for a wolf, so be careful you don't confuse him with a fox—he doesn't like that much. But being small always works to his advantage. You will hear Mischief howl when he is excited. "aaaaWHOOOOO!"

And we can't forget about the X-van, which takes the X-tails to the mountains, ocean, BMX tracks, and skateboard parks. This off-road machine can go anywhere and easily fits all of the X-tails' gear. Wisdom the Lion is always the driver of the X-van.

THE X-VAN

Kicking up dust, their dirt bikes rumbled in the valley . . .

They bounced, swerved and sped past dinosaurs. Not real dinosaurs, of course, but fossils hidden in the rocks. Grinning under their helmets, the X-tails were thrilled to dirt bike at Badlands!

Velociraptors, T. Rex and all kinds of dinosaurs had once lived at Badlands. Their footprints were still stamped in the ground.

Following the trail, Wisdom the Lion turned the throttle to go faster, but then slammed on the brakes. He had spotted something in the dirt.

Getting off his bike, the lion crouched down to investigate. "These look like dinosaur footprints, but they're fresh," said Wisdom, puzzled.

Charm the Kangaroo shook her head in disbelief. "Someone is playing a joke on us. They must be from an elephant. You do realize that dinosaurs are extinct, right?"

"Sure I do," laughed Wisdom. "But I can't explain these tracks."

"OOOHHHH, OOOHHHH, OOOHHHH!"

"Where do the footprints go?" grunted Flight the Gorilla. Without waiting for an answer, he rode off the trail to follow the mysterious tracks. The rest of the X-tails hurried to catch up, heading deeper into Badlands.

The footprints disappeared when they arrived at a roaring river. The X-tails saw that the water was smashing into a pile of rocks. Someone had built a bridge over the river, but there was one big problem: the rock bridge was working like a dam! The river was blocked and water was spilling into the valley.

Beyond the dam was a deep canyon. "That's where the river used to go," said Crash the Hippo, pointing at the bottom. Then he tilted his head to look closer.
"GaaaWHOOOOOMPHaaaaaa!
It's like a dinosaur museum down there!"

They carefully rode their dirt bikes down into the canyon. Fossils were everywhere. Even more exciting were the fresh footprints in the sand—the same ones they had followed earlier! Riding underneath dinosaur bones, the X-tails tracked the footprints to a dark cave.

Pulling headlamps out of their backpacks and putting them on, the friends went into a long tunnel where the river once flowed. It was eerily quiet, except for the sound of water dripping . . .

DRIP... DRIP... DRIP...

The X-tails crept forward on their bikes into the spooky tunnel . . .

CREEP... CREEP... CREEP...

Inside, bats fluttered and flapped around them . . .

The tunnel went on and on. Preparing to turn around, Mischief the Wolf saw daylight. "Holy animal crackers, Batman! Let's get out of this bat cave!" he howled, laughing.

Zooming out, they raced to the top of the canyon. Then they stopped and gawked. Trees towered to the clouds and the X-tails were like ants in the plants. It was a land for giants!

They had completely forgotten about the footprints that had brought them there—until they heard snarling! Looking up, they saw a gigantic nose breathing down on them!

The X-tails cowered behind Flight. The gorilla stood tall, acting brave, but his knees knocked and his lips quivered.

“Hello,” said a squeaky voice. “My name is Screech.”
Then out from behind the trees came a dinosaur—
Screech was a Tyrannosaurus Rex!

“What are you?” Screech asked, showing his razor teeth.
“You don’t look very tasty.”

“We’re the X-tails,” growled Dazzle, “and I’m a bear!

Screech looked at them suspiciously. He wasn't sure what an X-tail was. "Are you here to mess up Goodlands?"

"What do you mean?" asked Dazzle, confused.

"When I went to Badlands—where you came from—I saw garbage and mess and dirt where nothing grew," squeaked Screech. "I can't let that happen here in Goodlands. This is our home and we have to keep it safe."

"Why did you go to Badlands?" asked Dazzle. "Somebody could have seen you. If animals knew about you, that could be the end of Goodlands."

Screech dropped his head sadly.

“The tunnel you came through has always been filled with water. A few days ago, the river dried up, leaving us no fish to eat and nothing to drink. I went to see if I can turn the water back on . . . and I can. I will smash down that pile of rocks blocking the river! But before I do, I must say good-bye to my family and friends. After the tunnel fills with water, I won’t be able to come home.”

The X-tails stood in silence. Then Wisdom spoke up, “Maybe we can help.” He huddled with the others, whispering his plan.

Moments later, he looked up at Screech, who had been joined by more dinosaurs. They had come to see what the strangers were up to.

"We'll fix the river," said Wisdom. "Then your secret will be safe with us. Besides, no one would ever believe that we've met real dinosaurs!"

Screech smiled. "You would do that for us?"

"Of course," said Wisdom. "Goodlands is special. It needs to stay clean and beautiful."

"Before you leave," said Screech, glaring at the dirt bikes, "can my friends try those funny looking noise-makers?"

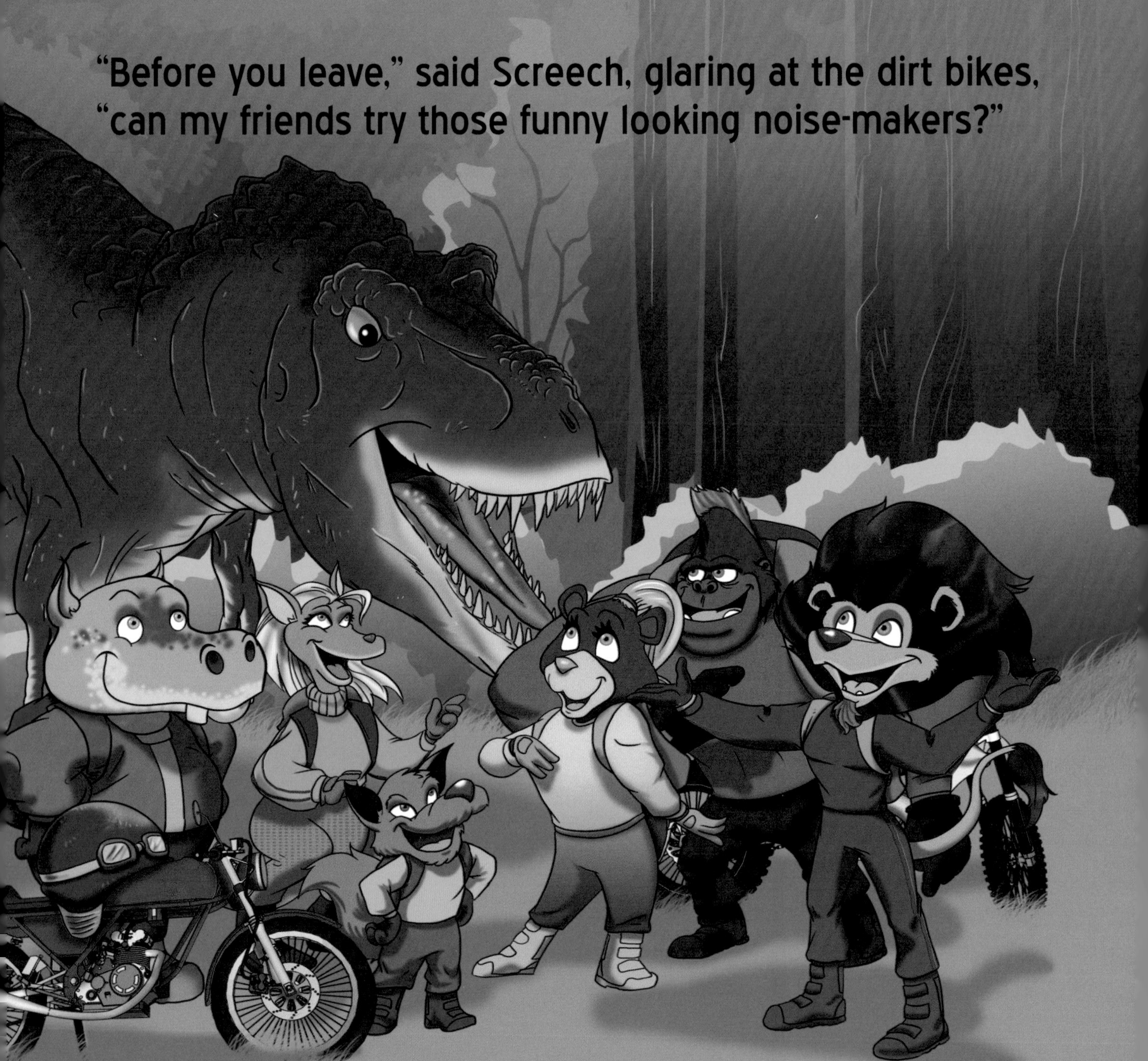

"Okay, but they might be too . . ." Before Mischief finished his sentence, the dinosaurs had grabbed the dirt bikes. Sitting down, the shocks SQUISHED and the seats SQUASHED. The X-tails did a safety check, showing them how to kick start, brake and turn the throttle to go. Preparing for wheelies, jumps and flying dirt, the dinosaurs cranked the throttles.

And do you know what happened?

The dinosaurs puttered along, slow as prehistoric snails.

“Thanks for the ride,” said the triceratops, “but we can walk faster than riding these bike dirts.”

Screech and the other dinosaurs all laughed and hugged their new friends good-bye.

The X-tails began the long ride through the tunnel and along the canyon.

When they reached the dam, they flexed their muscles: time to move rocks! They tied ropes to the big boulders and then hauled them out with their dirt bikes.

Soon, a trickle of water turned into a tidal wave
rushing down the canyon, filling the tunnel.

They pounded each other on the back, proud of their good deed, but then . . .

UH-OH.

"Hey, guys," thumped Charm. "We're on the wrong side of the river! How will we get back to our trail?"

Mischief grinned. "Wisdom's not the only smart one. I have an idea." He looked at the pile of rocks and the X-tails knew what he was thinking. The rocks they'd moved had created a dino-sized jump.

Quickly smoothing out the jump with dirt, they blasted over the river with zoober-super tricks:

HEEL CLICKER

and a

RULER!

When the X-tails got back to the trail, they stopped in amazement: garbage was everywhere on the ground. They hadn't noticed it earlier.

"What a mess!" said Charm. "If we cared more about the environment, Badlands would be clean and green like Goodlands. We sure made a lot of mistakes today. When we drove off the trail and went into the canyon, we hurt the dirt. I'm glad we fixed the river. And I hope whoever blocked the water won't make that mistake again, either."

As they went along the trail, the X-tails filled their packs with garbage. Picking up an empty juice box for recycling, Crash pointed at the ground. "Oh no, check this out!"

On the ground were fresh footprints—dinosaur prints!

"Screech sure got far when he was exploring Badlands," sighed Wisdom. "We'd better brush away all of his tracks to keep Goodlands safe. We learned a lot today, but the most important thing is . . ."

Mischief interrupted. "The most important thing is that we don't look tasty!" he giggled and the X-tails' laughter howled down the trail as they headed home.

THE TRICK-TIONARY

CLIFFHANGER

Launching off the jump, the rider stands up and rises into the air, only to catch the underside of the handlebars with their feet. The rider raises their hands high above their head as if riding a roller coaster. Before landing, the rider quickly sits back down on the bike. Charm the Kangaroo's big feet sure help with this trick!

FLINTSTONE

Take a step back in time with this trick. Sailing off the jump, the rider swings both legs to one side of the dirt bike. Then the rider begins to walk on air next to the bike while taking their hands off the handlebars. The last step is getting back on the bike. Every time Crash the Hippo lands this trick, he bellows, "Yabba Dabba Doooooo!"

Heel Clicker

Flying off the jump, the rider raises their feet above the handlebars. Continuing to hold onto the handlebars, the rider wraps their legs around their arms and clicks both heels together above the front tire. Just like Dorothy in The Wizard of Oz, Dazzle the Bear will sometimes wear ruby red slippers when performing this trick!

Nac-nac

When leaving the jump, the rider raises one leg and swings it behind them to the opposite side. The rider then puts their foot back on the peg for a perfect landing. With lots of practice at the dirt bike track, Charm the Kangaroo learned to Nac-nac!

Rock Solid

This trick is for experts only! High in the air, the rider does their best Superman impression. Holding on tightly to the seat with both hands, the rider kicks their feet behind the bike. Then the unthinkable happens—the rider lets go! Flying like a bird above the dirt bike, the rider grabs the seat to get back on. Mischief the Wolf lands this trick every time because he's solid as a rock!

When stopped or moving slowly, the rider cranks the throttle to spin the back tire. The force of the spinning tire will throw a cloud of dirt. Make sure no one is behind you when trying this trick or you'll be in big trouble!

STOPPIE

No air time needed for this trick. The rider carefully squeezes the front brake and leans forward, but not too far. The result is the back wheel lifts off the ground while the bike is ridden on the front wheel. Make sure you don't squeeze the brakes too hard or you'll fly head over tail!

While riding on the ground, the rider stands on the seat in a surfer position. The rider may let go with one hand or hold on with both hands depending on their experience level. Surf's up, dudes!

WHIP

When in the air, an experienced rider will whip their bike. The front of the bike is held straight and the back of the bike is swung to one side. The rider then straightens out the bike before landing. Once you learn to Whip, go celebrate with pie and whipping cream!

RULER

Launching off the jump, the rider extends their feet straight toward the sky in a handstand position. At the same time, the rider pushes the back of the bike straight down. Both the rider and bike are straight like a ruler. Wisdom the Lion is a master at the Ruler because . . . he rules!

L.A. FIELDING

L.A. Fielding is an author of children's literature and a member of the Canadian Authors Association. He dreamed up the X-tails for his two children, while telling stories on their long distance trips to the mountains each winter weekend. It is his family's cozy log home in Prince George, British Columbia, and their Fielding Shred Shack at a local ski resort, where he draws his inspiration.

Growing up skateboarding, biking, and snowboarding, L.A. Fielding now shares the fun of those sports with his family. When not writing or telling stories, he focuses his thoughts on forestry as a Registered Professional Forester. *The X-tails Dirt Bike at Badlands* is his seventh book in the X-tails series.

Other books in the series include:

- *The X-tails Snowboard at Shred Park*
- *The X-tails Skateboard at Monster Ramp*
- *The X-tails Ski at Spider Ridge*
- *The X-tails BMX at Thunder Track*
- *The X-tails Surf at Shark Bay*
- *The X-tails Travel to the Jamboree Jam*

WWW.THEXTAILS.COM